BEFORE VENGEANCE

VENGEANCE DEMONS BOOK 0
A NOVELLA

Louisa Lo

TIN CAN
PRESS

Cover Photo: Sara Eirew
Cover Design: Jacqueline Sweet
Editing: Joshua Essoe & Jena O'Connor
Beta Reading: Christie Stratos & Gina Grant
Interior Design: Tin Can Press

Before Vengeance/Louisa Lo—1st edition
ISBN: 978-0-9939396-3-1

To Austin.

ONE

Serafina

UNDER THE FADING SUN, I hurried past the palace square, keeping my shoulders slumped and my eyes downcast. To the conversing nobles in the vicinity, all they saw was a misfit. Someone looking to avoid trouble and attention.

The truth was, I was trying to avoid bringing attention to the trouble I might cause.

"Lady Serafina," Alston, the royal butler, called from behind me.

I whirled around on the smooth, white marble floor. Alston balanced a jug of honey in each hand. The lower grade honey was intended as payments to the brownies for their housekeeping service.

I tried to concentrate on Alston's words, and not the fact that the honey had been skimmed off the top by the butler.

Damn my keen sense of right and wrong, so utterly opposed to what everyone else on this plane considered normal.

"M'lady," the imposing butler seemed disgusted with himself for having to address me. He didn't even bother with a bow. "I'm to inform you that on the day of the Crossover, you're to come to the South Tower before dawn."

I nodded and started walking, hoping that would be all.

"One more thing," Alston blocked my path, his eyes dropped to my neck with deep disapproval. "May I remind you to wear the Eye of Sebille at all times. I cannot stress enough the importance of it."

A couple of noble ladies close by snickered at me, their laughter rang across the square like bells. Their pixies, taking cue from their mistresses, zoomed right by my braid rather than keeping a respectable distance.

I swallowed, my fingers brushed against my bare neck of their own accord. The Eye of Sebille was a long necklace with a bejeweled, egg-sized pendant. I hated wearing it. Not just because of its dead weight and sharp surface, but because of the mystery it represented.

In all my seventeen summers, I had never laid eyes on the Sebille family heirloom. Now, I was suddenly expected to wear it all the time. Why? Did it have something to do with my birthday?

When Alston passed by me, one of the honey jugs brushed against my arm. As the glass made contact with my exposed skin, sensations exploded though my system. It was as though in that moment, I could feel the hardship of the brownies, thankless servants little better than slaves. I felt their every yawn, every sore muscle, and every blister.

A brownie would have to work all year long just to get a single jug of cheap honey. To have over a third of it taken away by someone in a position of power...

It wasn't right.

The injustices they suffered crashed through me like a tidal wave, stealing my breath and making my fists clench. But when the torrent of indignation passed, what was left in its place was a dead calm.

As I watched Alston's retreating back, a song rose in me

like a long-forgotten nursery rhyme:

Honey, they say you never go bad.
Make an exception,
For he who made the brownies sad.

Before Alston reached the corner of the palace square, he doubled over with pain. He dropped the jugs and collapsed on the floor, curling into a fetal position. He groaned, his arrogant and formidable demeanor gone.

The jugs bounced off the marble floor and landed on a small wooden patio table nearby, without a crack to the glass or a single drop of honey spilling.

Somehow, I knew Alston was in for a long night of food poisoning, just like I knew the brownies, to whom the jugs belonged, would find the honey tasted twice as sweet as it normally would. I had no idea how I knew. I just did.

A crowd started to gather around the stricken man. A low murmur buzzed like bees amongst the pathetic sobs of the butler. The sounds shook me out of whatever trance I had been under, and my calmness evaporated in an instant. I left the scene with terror coursing through my veins, and I almost gave into the urge to break into a run.

Oh no, not again. What have I done?

For me, puberty had come and gone with my fae magic never making an appearance. I accepted that, along with the nasty whispers and dirty looks that came with being an Inadequate—a fae born without magical abilities. But in the past few months I could've sworn that I had come into some sort of power. Though if that were true, it wasn't like any magic I'd seen or heard of before.

In the beginning it was the little things. A merchant happened to break an antique vase in front of me after shortchanging a client. A violent fit of coughing befell a chambermaid as I listened to her spreading a juicy piece of gossip. Unlike regular fae magic, which gave one power over a specific *thing*, such as an element, my power seemed to be connected to a certain *event*—the existence of injustices. What happened just now supported that theory.

I shook my head. I couldn't have caused Alston to be sick. It had to be a happy coincidence that what happened to him was exactly what I'd wanted. I must've been desperate—I saw power in myself when there wasn't any.

A low horn blew, announcing the arrival of traders.

I stopped in my tracks and tilted my head to listen. The horn went on for quite a while, signaling a wide selection of goods available for trade. There would be offerings ranging from goblin jewelries and Ambrosian perfume to human computer gadgets, all poached from their respective planes as proudly bragged by the traders.

Stolen goods. Theft. More injustices.

Such delicious injustices. Begging to be addressed. Maybe I could get all those goods to turn to dust, or better yet, turn them against their sellers. Think of the irony of a pair of goblin earrings chasing after the traders and poking them on the behind...

No, I told the part of me that was itching to spring into action. I reminded myself where I was headed before Alston interrupted me.

There would always be unfairness. There would always be wrongs. For tonight, there was only one I sought to right.

Two

Eldon

As I WALKED THROUGH THE palace ground in the warm early evening air, I could see that the preparations for the upcoming festivity were well under way.

Ingredients for the royal banquet were being brought into the Mirage Palace by the cartload, and the air was filled with the smell of salted meat, cheeses and spices. In the North Tower, Firwig, the Chief Elf and resident pyrotechnician, oversaw the loading of gunpowder into fireworks that promised to light up the entire land. At every corner of Dualsing, commoners' children eagerly bit into unicorn yogurt candies, a treat distributed in the queen's name. A taste of many more goodies to come.

It was a celebration where no detail was overlooked, yet the least important person involved was the birthday girl herself.

Reaching the stairs leading up to the Third Battlement, I stepped onto the dark landing and sent my senses out. When I was sure that I hadn't been followed, I began the long trek up the curving stone stairs, my defective right leg protesting every step of the way.

When I got to the top, I found Finny curled up in a crenel, watching the happenings on the palace grounds below as the last rays of sunset left the horizon. As always, the sight of her invoked a strong sense of protectiveness in me. Ironic, given she was whole and I was the one who was broken.

Bracing my hands on the coarse stone frame, I took a moment to get my bearings.

My heart skipped a beat when Finny spoke in a quiet voice. "The third step down."

"What?"

"The third step down is hollow. It gave you away."

Princes in general were not supposed to say words like "oops," or "dammit," let alone a crown prince in the fae kingdom of Dualsing. So I fired a question instead. "Why did you send for me? Is something wrong?"

As soon as the words left my mouth, I realized they sounded rather harsh. Last time we met, I told Finny I had to be out of touch for a while. There was so little time before the Crossover, and I needed every moment to set my game pieces in place or all would be lost.

I approached Finny as she got off the floor slowly. With large, solemn eyes, she looked at me for a long moment. When her eyes swept over my royal dress uniform, I stood a little taller, painfully conscious of the deformity of my leg that the rigid cut of my outfit was meant to hide.

"It's over, Eldon." She cupped my chin with her hand lightly, her touch soft as a feather, "It's high time I end this. Whatever *this* is."

She lowered her hand.

I was shocked. But really what did I expect after years of lying to her? "Finny, you know I hold you in the highest esteem."

I did. But until I could carry out my plan to secure the

throne, to become more than the crown prince in name only, I couldn't protect her properly. Until then, it would be foolish to acknowledge our relationship. I glanced down at her neck. At least that accursed pendant wasn't there.

I wanted Finny, but I wanted the crown too. And I had a plan that could get me both.

"Finny—"

She winced as if I'd punched her. "Stop calling me Finny!"

I'd been calling her Finny since she was four and I was five. As children, we would hide from the adults on this very battlement. We played chess, read books to each other, and puzzled over her family's coldness toward her. Then I turned sixteen and was let in on the Secret, the age-old ritual that would see Finny gone from my life once she reached adulthood.

That was why her eighteenth birthday celebration was called the Crossover. There would be no coming back from it. She had been kidnapped from her real parents when she was an infant. She was to stay in Dualsing until she turned eighteen, then she would leave. End of story. Meanwhile, she suffered endless I-know-something-you-don't-know snickers as everyone above the age of sixteen in our world was fully aware of her fate.

The day I was told the Secret was the day I started pulling away from her. At least publicly.

But our meetings on the battlement continued, under many layers of cloaking enchantments. And I started the long road to finding a way to prevent the Crossover from happening.

"Soon I'll be able to explain everything to you. I just need a little more time—"

"You've been saying that for a long time now. Enough is enough. You're ashamed of us, admit it."

I let out an exasperated sigh, though princes should never show weakness by sighing or becoming exasperated. I couldn't be honest with her. Her life, my crown, and everything else depended on it. I rubbed my face and sat down on the rough stone floor, my pristine, white outfit be damned. I patted the space next to me. "Sit with me. Please. We'll work through this."

Maybe I could stall her for another few weeks. By then I would be ready.

It was her turn to sigh. "Eldon, there's more than just *us* that is wrong. Everything else is, too, and you know it."

"All the more reason we should talk about it." I attempted a smile though I was panicking on the inside.

Tell me what you suspect. Tell me what you've already figured out. I need to know how close you are to the truth.

Something about my words caused a change in her. To my alarm, Finny started quivering, her thick, brown braid shaking in sync with the rest of her body. She took large gulping breaths as if she was having a hard time taking air into her lungs.

I jumped and grabbed her arm. "What's happened? What have they done to you?"

"Talk about it?" Finny gave an incredulous laugh that didn't sound like her at all, her eyes flashing. "What can we talk about? You're not only keeping *us* a secret from others, you're keeping things from *me* as well."

I bit my lip.

I realized too late that Finny was trembling with rage, not fear or sadness. I didn't even know she could get angry like that. She'd always been my sweet and gentle Serafina. I did not recognize this fierce and indignant young woman glaring daggers at me.

And it looked like she had only just started.

"You want to talk? Where shall we start? How about the fact that only today I was given the first piece of information about my own birthday celebration, and that was nothing more than an instruction about where to go the morning of? The planning for this began months ago."

Finny gestured to the palace grounds spread out before us. Servants bustled about, carrying wine and bedding for five hundred guests, blissfully unaware of the unfolding drama above. "In two weeks I'm to have a massive, nation-wide festival planned in my name, and no one will tell me what the celebration is truly about. Granted, I am the daughter of an earl, but there are more than two dozen earls in Dualsing and most of them have children. Why am I the only one getting this honor?"

"Finny," I began, but didn't know what else to say, and it looked like she didn't expect me to go on.

"Even before I became an Inadequate, they didn't like me. They never have. Not my parents. Not anyone else in this palace. I know that and I've accepted it. But this, this farce...why? Haven't I already been enough of a laughing stock?"

How could I forget how Finny hated being the center of attention? All this pomp and circumstance was putting her on display like a show unicorn. I was too focused on what the humans called the endgame.

"None of this is about me," she stated flatly. "If it was, someone would've gone through the full itinerary of the day with me already. If it was really about me, I would've gotten a visit from Madame Sutura by now."

Finny was far too perceptive for her own good. It was true that everyone from the humble footman to the Lord Chamberlain had already had their measurements taken by the royal seamstress for the matching fineries prepared just for the occasion.

I could neither confirm nor deny her claim; all I could do was back up against the wall while Finny advanced on me. "Why, then? What's going on? If it's really about me," her voice shook now, "why does Mother stall every time I ask her about the Trip?"

The Trip. A once-in-a-lifetime chance for Dualsingians to see the world, meant to be taken right after they became adults. Finny and I used to talk about taking ours together. Back before I knew that it would never be. I had turned eighteen almost a year ago, and had been making one excuse after another to delay it. I dared not take the Trip, afraid that they would send Finny away while I was gone.

"Well say something!" We were almost nose to nose now. "Or don't. You won't tell me the truth anyway."

At first I thought the tightness in my throat was an involuntary response to the glimpse of fear I saw lurking behind the fury in her eyes, then, to my horror, I realized that I couldn't breathe. An invisible fist held my windpipe in a death grip, and the air seethed with the presence of magic. Not fae power, but something darker.

And it was coming from Finny.

What did she say to me? *Well say something! Or don't.*

With those fateful words she had unintentionally cut off my airway. She was no Inadequate, yet the power she'd come into wasn't that of the fae.

Because *she* was not fae.

I opened my mouth but no sound came out. My body

grew heavy.

Then I saw it.

With the next burst of her power, a pair of wings sprouted at her back. They were gray in color, covered in tiny scales that gave off a pearl-like luster in the dark.

Definitely not fae wings.

Two words echoed in my head as my world turned dark.

Vengeance demon.

THREE

Serafina

ONE MOMENT I WAS YELLING at Eldon in a bitter tone I couldn't even recognize myself, the next he was turning blue right before my eyes.

Oh no, no! Did I do that? All the pent-up rage and frustration was turning me into a bag of explosives, all it took was getting a little worked up to have an outburst.

I pillowed his head with my arm just before he hit the floor. His fingers, clawing at his throat to no avail, started to sag. Out of pure instinct, I placed my hands over them and searched within myself for the power to push air into his lungs.

But he's toying with you. The part of me that was refusing to relinquish the control of his airways fumed.

Let go. Now! I pushed aside my *other* voice and forced Eldon's chest to rise, then fall. Then rise and fall again.

He coughed and spit like a drowning man rescued.

"Finny." He opened his eyes but his voice was weak.

I shifted his head onto my lap, anger at him temporarily abated. Almost accidentally killing someone had a way of making one feeling more kindly toward them. I caressed his hair, not wanting this moment to pass, but knowing it had to for his sake.

I removed one of his cuff links and raised my arm to throw it into the air. Quick as lightening, Eldon grabbed hold of my hand.

"What are you doing?" he demanded.

"You know what I'm doing. Calling for help." In an emergency, the cuff links could be made to brighten and float in midair, serving the same beaconing function as a human flare gun.

I knew what calling for help meant. It meant having my new power discovered, for there was no question now that I did possess it. Every fiber in my being was telling me to keep it hidden, but Eldon's well-being came first. I might be hurt over his handling of our relationship, but I did love him. And he was on the floor because of me.

After pocketing his cuff links, Eldon reached for the corner of a crenel, using it to pull himself up. The rough stone tore at his sleeve. "I'm fine. Whatever it is, it's passed."

"But—"

"Don't worry about it. I skipped dinner. I'm a bit low on energy, and I fainted. That's all." He winked at me. "I am to drink with General Tok tonight. Can you blame me for not wanting to eat beforehand?"

I narrowed my eyes. I'd been lied to by Eldon enough to know when he was doing it again. The attempted joke. The forcefully cheerful wink. The purposeful omitting of his suffocation.

Under my stare, Eldon sighed, looking more exhausted than I'd ever seen him. "All right. I didn't just faint. You nearly killed me. You have an unfamiliar power with zero guidance on how to control it. You have a voice inside you telling you to turn into some kind of justice seeker. Is that closer to the truth?"

My mouth fell open.

"Finny..." He touched his forehead to mine. "The fact that I know all this and I'm still telling you to lie low, does it not mean something? Can you, please, please, ask me no more?"

In the end, it wasn't the shock of the confession that made me nod. It wasn't even the creepiness of having my fierce inner voice so accurately described.

It was Eldon's face—the dark purple blotches staining the skin beneath his eyes. I could see them plainly now since he'd dropped his glamour at the same time he'd dropped his act.

We looked at each other, not sure what to say. Then we spoke at the same time.

"I'm sorry I lost my temper," I said.

"I'm sorry I lied to you," he said.

But he was still lying. I intended to find out more, but right now I didn't want to fight with him.

I knew deep down that our time on the battlement was coming to an end.

Eldon conjured an orb of pure energy on his palm and pulled bright blue lines out of it as if it was a ball of yarn. With a snap of his fingers, the lines rearranged themselves into a checkerboard pattern, hovering just above the floor. Next came the semi-transparent game pieces in the shapes of pawns, bishops, knights, rooks, kings, and queens.

Pure, undiluted energy had always been his power.

"You wanna play?" He struggled out of his tailcoat, the process made difficult by sitting and by its ridiculous length. Tossing it aside, he rolled up the sleeves of his white dress shirt.

Reluctantly, I smiled. "What about General Tok?"

"He can wait."

Four

Serafina

I MADE MY WAY TO the observatory in the east wing of the palace, passing through a section of the hallway with an open roof. Eldon and I had managed two rounds of chess before I had to report for duty. I'd missed my nap before my night shift, but I wouldn't have been able to rest after all that adrenaline had coursed through my body anyway.

I'd used my new power twice in a night. I'd allowed my destructive impulses to stir my blood, and Eldon almost paid for it with his life. Never mind that he'd been lying to me about my magic. He didn't deserved to be killed by it.

A firefly-eagle, a creature with the body of an eagle and the glow of a firefly, cried overhead. I looked up, following its flight over the palace grounds to the snow-capped mountain just beyond the castle's walls.

Then I spotted the predator's target—a white mountain goat making its way up the face of a cliff. I tried to look away, but it was too late.

With momentum on its side, the firefly-eagle hurtled toward the hoofed animal, knocking it off balance. The poor goat fell from the cliff. It landed in the valley where the walls of the palace began, breaking its neck. The firefly-eagle picked up the fresh corpse and went on its way.

Dinner was served.

I shuddered. Though the same scene repeated itself on a frequent basis, it never made witnessing it any less disturbing. Many palace residents liked to make book on the firefly-eagle's success rate, but I found the scene gruesome. In addition to the whole situation with Eldon, it was enough to make me want to crawl under the covers of my bed and not get up for a week.

I would dearly love to shirk my duties for the night, but I was hoping my work could provide some answers.

Mother had always said that working at the observatory was a gift, but I didn't have that much faith in the statement. I wasn't sure what teenage noblewomen from other realms were like, but in my world, they did not often work in an isolated section of the palace on the midnight shift.

But I was different; I was the awkward, never-quite-accepted daughter of Lord and Lady Sebille.

It wasn't even the hard work that I minded, it was the growing conviction that whatever was going on in my life, working at the observatory was a part of it.

It was in the averted eyes I encountered from servants and nobles alike, the halted forward motion when they realized I was in the hallway heading to work, the slight lift of the corners of their mouths—or in some rare cases—the look of sympathy, hastily masked.

I could take the mockery, but it was the pity that unsettled me the most.

And being unsettled and frustrated was dangerous. Just look at the shameful way I'd behaved when that anxiety blossomed into anger.

I lowered my head and quickened my steps. Though the

possibility of encountering anyone at this hour was slim, I didn't want to take the chance. Not only because my emotions were still raw, but because in the midst of all that restlessness and unease, my heart sang.

It didn't matter that Eldon wasn't completely honest with me. It didn't matter that just hours ago I was ready to cut ties with him once and for all. It didn't even matter that I'd almost killed him. When he formed the chess pieces out of that energy orb and we settled into a game that kept our minds busy but our souls at peace, I knew that times like that would be no more.

My heart had been glowing, not because I was naïve and optimistic, but because I knew the moment would not last. I wanted to hold onto the warmth that had spread inside me for as long as I could.

My footsteps resounding in the deserted stone hallway, I could tell that I'd reached the east wing by the sudden dimness of my surroundings. Everywhere else, the countless drops of Molten Amber embedded in the walls grew bright to guide night travelers throughout the palace. It was what the Mirage Palace was famous for, and why the gems' native plane had since gone barren from over-mining.

While the Mirage Palace was a structure of quartz and white marble that any self-respecting fae would deem magnificent, its east wing stood out by its very absence of grandeur and magic.

The east wing had no eternal fountains. No oasis of ever-blooming phoenix orchids. No unicorns grazing in its courtyard. In fact, there was no word to describe this part of the palace except "functional," which was about the most indecent word one could employ in Dualsing. In this unfashionable part of the palace, the walls stayed dark; the passages had flat, low ceilings; and there was not even a single ornamental statue.

I turned a corner, passed a long row of plain wooden doors, and stopped in front of the last one. I opened the door and went up a long, narrow flight of stairs, aided only by a couple of weak, mounted oil lamps and a shaky set of handrails. Stale air and the burnt smell of animal fat assaulted my nose while the squeaky sound of the rickety stairs amplified in the quiet surrounding. At the top of the stairs was another door, and the observatory I was assigned to lay behind it. The whole place was designed to block any foreign light source that might be disruptive to the monitoring and recording business conducted inside.

I opened the door a crack and asked tentatively, "Mr. Lichen?"

"Come on in, m'lady," a deep voice boomed.

I entered the observatory, closing the door behind me. Though I'd been coming here for almost a year now, I had never quite gotten over the sense of wonder when I entered the three-story structure. Eldon once told me that the human plane had structures that were similar to this called IMAX theaters, except they weren't powered by magic, but technology.

In the hushed darkness, the only source of light was from the dome-shaped ceiling above. Mesmerizing bright lines, similar to the ones Eldon created for our chess games but in multiple colors, shaped and reshaped themselves into overlapping patterns on a backdrop of royal blue.

Mr. Lichen got up from the desk at the center of the room, gesturing toward the three heavy volumes he'd already pulled out for me. "Tonight it's Eglantina-Six,

Marigold-Twelve, and Oda-Four. Now that you're here, I'll be on my way."

I nodded, knowing my mentor would have no trouble seeing my gesture despite the lack of light. After a lifetime of working here, he had developed an uncanny ability to see in the dark. I waited until the door closed behind him with a thump before letting out a shaky breath, though whether my reaction was due to the cool air or my assigned task, I knew not.

I reached the desk. "Alina, are you there?"

Alina, a pixie, zoomed in front of my face with an abundance of energy, her rapid-fire chatter even faster than the beating of her wings. She darted all over the place, doing spins and somersaults, then a mock dive bomb, the lantern in her hand threatening to go out with all the acrobatic moves.

"I-missed-you-how-have-you-been-has-it-really-been-a-day-since-you've-been-here-what-are-we-doing-tonight?"

I couldn't help but laugh. "Slow down!"

Alina clutched her chest in an imitation of heart failure and took a few deep breaths. "I. Miss. You. How. Have. You. Been? Going. This. Slow. Is. Killing. Me."

"Well, maybe not as slow as that," I said dryly.

Taking that as a point of victory, Alina shot up a few feet and did another couple of somersaults with a loud, "Yay-I-am-wearing-you-down!" before settling down on the surface of the desk. She sat, the long-suffering lantern on its side next to her.

"So, how have you been?" she asked.

"Fine," I lied. No way would I darken the little pixie's mood with my own problems.

Alina didn't look entirely convinced, but true to the

nature of her kind, she couldn't hold her suspicion, nor her attention, for long.

"Oh, I almost forgot!" she cried and flew into a half-opened drawer. She came back out hugging an enameled egg, its silver chain dangling off her feet. Her tiny arms could not even cover the entire circumference of the pendant, and the diamonds encrusted on its surface cut into her tender flesh.

I opened my palm and Alina dropped her offering into it right away, rubbing her skin.

"The Eye of Sebille," she breathed. "As you wish."

"Did they give you a hard time for retrieving it?"

"On the contrary, once my ma realized I was taking it to you, she was totally all right with it."

Alina's mother was pixie to one of the queen's ladies-in-waiting. Whatever the reason, they really wanted that piece of jewelry on me.

Maybe wearing it would help me figure out why. In the absence of a lot of leads, one must explore all of them.

By the time I finished securing the clasp behind my neck, Alina had moved on to examining the thick volumes stacked on the desk. Even standing, she wasn't as tall as a single one of the books.

"So, new records to update tonight, huh?"

"Yeah. Let's get right on it." I pulled at the neckline of my dress, hoping to get comfortable with the heavy pendant between my breasts, knowing full well it was futile. Prolonged wearing of the necklace always gave me a migraine.

I opened the wide book with the word *Eglantina* on its spine, and by the faint lantern light, flipped the thick, yellowed paper until I reached section six. There were three

tables there, one page each, titled using human Greek
letters "Alpha," "Beta," and "Gamma." Next to each name,
glued onto the page, was a small, intricate, rope-knot
charm constructed from a single strand of hair. The first
two knots were blond while the third was obviously
donated by a redhead.

My job was to update these tables with information
gauged from the dome, though I wasn't told much beyond
that.

I thought I had a good idea though. I believed that
Alpha, Beta, and Gamma were individuals I was assigned to
track—the hair charms certainly seemed to support that
theory—and Eglantina-Six was codename for the plane
where they were located. Then after I was done with
Eglantina-Six, it was onto Marigold-Twelve and Oda-Four,
each with their own set of tagged individuals.

In all the time I'd been here though, I'd never been asked
to track the whereabouts of those on Eglantina-Six, until
now.

I waved my hand at the illuminated patterns on the
dome and said, "Show me Eglantina-Six."

I had command over what was projected on the dome
not through fae magic, but human technologies Mr. Lichen
imported then reconfigured with magic. Dualsing, despite
its fantastic environment and otherworldly creatures, did
not stay in the Medieval age as its palace suggested. Its
citizens bragged that they took the best of every plane and
made it their own.

Stolen goods and all.

The mass juxtaposition of patterns on the dome faded
into the background until all but one remained, and
another wave from me caused it to magnify. The pattern

consisted of lines, circles, and rectangular shapes.

Alina's face turned upward. "I think we've got mountains for this round, don't you agree?"

Though Mr. Lichen refused to confirm that the patterns were three-dimensional geographic maps, there was no doubt in my mind that they were. In the past year I'd observed over a hundred patterns of layered contour lines, with markers indicating bodies of water and faemade structures.

Or *not* faemade structures, depended on what plane was actually being observed. So far, I'd seen worlds of water, underground mazes or castles in the sky. None of them were places we'd ever heard the adults discussing.

I'd always shared my speculations with Alina, but tonight some instinct urged me not to tell her my growing suspicion that what we had been working on at the observatory might tie back to the bigger mystery that was my life. I didn't want to get the sweet pixie into trouble. So I made a noncommittal sound at her comment and bent my head to the book.

"What's with you tonight?" Alina crossed her arms, pouting.

"I...eh...just want to get the job done and go home, that's all. I've been tired."

"I tried asking my ma about the patterns, you know," she said slyly.

That got my attention. "What did she say?"

"She won't tell me anything." Alina rolled her eyes. "Just keeps promising that I'll know when I get older."

When I get older. Like how Eldon got older and knew. I wondered what it was that everyone seemed to know—everyone except the very young and me.

I wondered if my little friend would start avoiding me too, once she joined the club of knowledge in a few years.

Alina was determined to ignore my excuse for not wanting to talk. She swept her arm over her head, encompassing the entire dome. "We're looking at some pretty strange mountains. Look how rectangular they all are, no matter how big or small. And those rock faces? They are sheer drops."

For someone who grew up in Dualsing, a world comprised of such aesthetically unpleasing rectangular blocks was even less plausible than a castle in the sky.

I knew what those mountains were.

Human buildings.

While the people of Dualsing were quick to embrace the inventions of those non-magical folks, humans' natural environment was not something they cared about or talked about. To Dualsingians, it mattered not what other planes were like, only what could be taken from them. I only knew what the human structures looked like because Eldon told me about them. Being disabled and at a disadvantage all his life, he had an interest in what many considered the weaker races.

"Let's get to work," I told Alina. "Talking is not going to get our job done any faster."

"All right." Alina sighed. "I'll get it out of you later. For now I'll keep quiet while you get the anchor ready."

"Thank you."

I closed my eyes and cleared my mind. Mr. Lichen had taught me the Reveal, a fae ability that could be learned even if one wasn't born with the natural talent. The Reveal allowed me to see the true condition of something through the visualization of a solid anchor. The anchor didn't have to be a physical object, but it had to have a personal meaning to the user.

An image of Eldon flew into my mind—his forehead wrinkled in contemplation as it had been just hours ago as he rolled a bishop between his fingers. It made me smile because whatever might come, it was a moment to be cherished. I focused my energy on that transparent bishop, on every line and curve that formed that chess piece.

With my anchor secured and my eyes squeezed shut, I fumbled at the pages of the text in front of me until I had one rope-knot charm pulsing under each palm. The redheaded knot lay beneath my left palm, its position in the text committed in my memory. I bridged the energies between the bishop and the rope knot charms. It mattered not that I wasn't physically touching all three of them—not when my anchor was based on a memory so recent.

When I opened my eyes and I could still see the bishop, I knew that I'd gotten it. I withdrew my hands from the rope-knot charms.

Without a word, Alina blew out the candle inside her lantern, and I lifted my head and drew the bishop over the pattern on the dome in slow motion as if it were a paintbrush. As the Reveal passed over each section of the pattern, it would fade by a shade or two. And then suddenly the tip of the bishop found what it had been seeking—a spot on the pattern grew bright instead of dim, then another, then another.

By the time Alina gave light to the lantern again with a snap of her fingers, there were three glowing dots above us.

Alpha, Beta, and Gamma.

Dots like these had been in my dreams since I started at the observatory, their bright lights dancing and twinkling in my mind's eye, their voices whispered of longing. Of not belonging. Like me.

I never told Eldon what I had been working on at the observatory, nor did I tell him about the dreams. Yet it was indeed the dreams that first got me thinking that those hair charms in the record books represented real people. I felt such an unexplainable connection with them, like we were kin somehow. Not kin like how all nobility were related in one way or another, but a deeper tie. Some shared destinies.

Maybe it wasn't a coincidence that I was the only one among my peers who was assigned to the observatory. Maybe I was given the job because there was something in me that made finding my charges easier.

Like recognized like.

And yes, I'd come to think of those whom the dots might be depicting as my charges.

Who are they? Why are they being tracked? Why is tracking them the only time I was ever taught non-talent-based magic?

Something suspicious was happening here.

The dots lit up yellow. That was a good sign, though Mr. Lichen never explained why that was so. If my theory was right, and the pattern was depicting a human city, then Alpha seemed to be on the ground level between two structures, Beta was in a two-story house, and Gamma was pacing on top of a tall building.

Pulling out a jar of ink and a feather pen from the drawer under the table, I began carefully writing down the locations of the three dots on the record book and their relative positions to each other. The tables for Alpha and Beta were only half filled, while Gamma's were onto the second-to-last line of the page. My next job was to compare the data to the last entry for the trio from three months ago, logged by Mr. Lichen himself, judging from the handwriting.

All three were within the parameters of their respective "home bases," as directed by the record book, but Gamma was almost at the apex of the boundary due to the height of its current position.

I traced my fingertips over Gamma's table. I looked up at the dome and stared at Gamma's glow of light. There was something both fascinating and terrifying about it, more so than any of the other dots I'd encountered. I'd never worked on Eglantina-Six, and by extension, Gamma, before tonight. Yet it was like a forgotten dream, achingly familiar and frustratingly foreign.

I'd come to the observatory hoping for answers, but I was at a loss on how to proceed.

Then I felt the pendent grow hot, and the discomfort that came with wearing it blossomed into a sharp migraine.

And all hell broke loose.

FIVE

Eldon

"**I** SAW."

The soft words coming from a figure leaning against the passage stopped me in my tracks. I was making my way to General Tok, who was staying at the guest residence. He was most likely already into the third bottle of fae wine and cursing my tardiness to Hell and back, but this was one delay I couldn't afford to ignore.

Foster, the ne'er-do-well youngest son of a minor noble and an unapologetic gossipmonger, gestured me to move into a shadowy corner off the passage. I did so with deliberate slowness, making sure that no one saw us go in together. Being this close to the central square, there were plenty of fae milling around, chatting, laughing, and politically maneuvering in anticipation of Finny's so-called celebration. Exotic perfume, worn by both women and men, aimed to beguile the senses of their intended target.

Anything for a trinket or a useful piece of information.

"Greetings, Foster." I kept my voice neutral despite the pounding of my heart. *How much does he know?*

"Don't play games with me." Foster smirked. "I saw that little deviant calling her power when I flew patrol earlier."

My cloaking enchantment was meant to conceal our

presence, but Finny's surge of energy must've broken through it, leaving Foster privy to what happened on the battlement.

"You would've seen me, too, Your Royal Highness. But oh, wait, you were too busy fainting."

No use clarifying that I hadn't so much fainted away as I had been almost choked to death. It would not help Finny's case.

"What do you want?" I used the most direct approach because there was no use trying to demand the respect that Foster was required to show as per royal protocols—everyone knew I was the heir apparent in name only.

"Did you see her wings? They aren't fae wings, that's for sure."

Finny's wings had always been there, but they were enchanted to hide themselves, even from their owner, until after the Crossover. But her outburst must've brought them out pre-maturely.

"We both know what she is. So I ask you again, what do you want?"

"It's not what I want. It's what *you* want. If you want me to keep quiet, then you'd better give me—"

I didn't wait to hear Foster outline his terms because whatever they were, he would not honor them. The queen would find out about Finny's ability and move up her schedule of removal from Dualsing, leaving me with no time to prevent the Crossover from happening.

In the precious seconds that talking to Foster had used, I had rubbed my fingertips over the potent, emergency fairy dust I'd planted on the side seam of my pants where my hands naturally fell. The general-purpose magic enhancer could be a game changer in a dire situation.

When Foster started naming his terms, I encased him in a prison of pure energy, my natural strength multiplied by the fairy dust by tenfold.

By the time Foster blasted through my energy prison with his own magic, I had already made a mental call to the Molten Amber embedded in the walls. The amber, multiple separate entities with one hive-minded consciousness, congregated around the shadowy corner with the grace of a school of fish in a rapid current.

I pushed Foster toward the wall, and the Molten Amber pulled him into it. They placed themselves all over the fae's body, enveloping him in a confinement of orange glow. Then the light dimmed until the wall looked like it was no different from any of its neighbors.

Individually the Molten Amber could be easily crushed by a fae, but their collective strength could overpower someone of mid-level magic, like Foster, for a time.

No one suspected that I had formed a strategic alliance with beings they perceived as magically less superior. To the fae of Dualsing, a people of generational thieves and deceivers, there were only two types of beings outside their kind: the more intelligent ones they had to figure out how to fool, and the less intelligent ones they took advantage of outright. Being looked down upon all my life because of my disability and my joke of a claim to the throne, I had developed a knack for picking up on the discontent of others. One night a year ago, I'd listened to the low humming in the walls, the sad song of the Molten Amber as it lamented the day it had been unearthed from its natural habitat to serve the people of Dualsing. Answering that outcry with gentle understanding and comradeship had earned me the unwavering loyalty of a valuable ally.

These walls really did have ears, after all.

And they collected secrets on my behalf.

If I could not become the true heir to the throne through pure physical prowess, then I intended to be a thousand times as cunning to compensate. I'd learned early on that information was the road to true power.

I did a quick calculation in my head and figured I'd bought myself two weeks, maybe three. That was how long the Molten Amber could hold someone of Foster's magical ability in stasis.

Through my friends within the walls, I knew that Foster and his superior butted heads over Foster's work ethics—or lack thereof. Also, his intended was stepping out with someone who worked in the same kitchen she did. With a few carefully chosen words whispered in the right ears, I could make it look as if Foster had somehow found out about the affair and took off in a huff. It would not be completely out of character for the undependable fae to simply disappear without informing his boss.

And by the time Foster's absence started to become suspicious, Finny's big celebration would be over, and it wouldn't have mattered one way or the other. Either my plan would work and my sin would be overlooked or my plan would fail and there would be plenty of hell to pay as it was. What was one more crime?

I walked as fast as my limp would allow, trying not to look like I was hurrying away.

Trust, my miniature dragon the size of a large wolfhound, caught up with me halfway through the central square. A fae hurried past us, almost knocking Trust over, not bothering to give the aging dragon any personal space. Given the sight of Trust's winkled and dry-looking wings, many ignored the presence of the once-noble beast.

"I know, I know. I'm on my way," I said to Trust without much enthusiasm, assuming he was there to tell me to hurry up for my engagement with General Tok. I would dearly love to avoid the engagement, but being late was one thing, being a no-show was completely another. I had to forge onward, though I was in no mood for the military man's boasting of battle glories, which were more about recounting tales of getting away with gross deceptions and evading justice than true bravery.

Though, in truth, evading justice *was* the Dualsingian definition of true bravery.

Trust butted his scaled head in my stomach, stopping me.

"What is it, old man?"

Trust looked around him, indicating that we weren't alone. He was mute to the rest of Dualsing, but not to me. He might be reluctant to speak in front of an audience, but there was no mistaking the urgency in his eyes.

"What is it?" I asked again softly, trying to crouch down to his level as much as my weaker leg would allow.

Trust tilted his head toward the observatory, walked toward that direction, then paced back to me.

Finny.

Six

Serafina

ONE MOMENT I WAS MESMERIZED by Gamma's eerie glow, the next its yellow light was turning crimson.

Sheer terror invaded my being, not simply from the training drilled into me that the color crimson at the observatory was very bad news, but because of the sudden winter chill settling into my bones. I slid onto the floor and hugged my body, shaking. I couldn't talk, couldn't think. I clenched my jaw to keep my teeth from rattling.

And my pounding headache continued.

"Call...Mr. Lich...Lichen," I managed to tell an alarmed Alina before slipping away...

...into a world of starless sky, glass and bright lights.

Part of me knew I wasn't really there—wherever this place was. I was floating in midair, a passing crow flew over my body—no, *through* my body. I held up my hands—they were translucent.

I could just make out a meandering path of flashing, moving mechanical boxes below, and in front of me was the rooftop of a thirty-story building I'd only ever heard Eldon describe with words. The building was one in a sea of over a hundred, stretching from one side of the city to the other, its brilliant lights blinding me like a million candles.

I couldn't feel the migraine anymore, nor the cold for that matter, but my guts felt like ice just the same.

Was this really a dream? If so, how could I dream about a place I'd never visited in such vivid detail? And if I was indeed dreaming, should I not have taken everything at face value?

A movement caught my eyes.

Two girls dressed in dark, form-fitting outfits were arguing on the rooftop. The older one had waist-length dark hair, the other one, who seemed to be the same age as me, had short, red hair that danced around her face like a flame.

The vibrant color reminded me of the hair charm I touched just a little while ago.

Red hair. Gamma.

I'd seen her in my dreams many times before. Dreams that weren't meant to be remembered in the glaring day of light. Could the connection I felt with her have propelled my spirit to cross dimensions? To seek the answers about my life I'd been looking for?

If my theory was right, and the pattern was depicting a human city, then Alpha seemed to be on the ground level between two other structures, Beta was in a two-story house on the other side of the city, and Gamma was pacing on top of a tall building.

If this was the top of the building I envisioned when I first saw the pattern on the dome, then one of the girls below me was Gamma.

I had no idea who the girl beside Gamma was. According to the map, Alpha and Beta were in other parts of the city, so she couldn't have been one of them.

Another crow flew through my body, reminding me of my body-less status. Before I could process the mounting evidence that I had astral projected myself into another plane, a voice echoed in my head, the tone cold and angry. From the enraged look on the face of the flame-hair girl below, I had a feeling I knew whose inner thoughts I was listening to.

Not that mindreading was an everyday occurrence for me, but then again, neither was astral travelling.

That fucking blade is mine now, and she better leave me be if she knows what's good for her.

"Give it back, Anastasia!" the dark haired girl demanded. "You'll earn your own when you graduate from Vengeance U. *If* you graduate."

"But I like this one, Gab." Anastasia smiled and stroked the iron dagger in her gloved hand.

My knee-jerk reaction was to move back, away from the deadly blade. In Dualsing, iron was a fearsome word whispered in hushed tones. It rendered many human products unsuitable for import.

"It's Cousin Gabriella to you. Don't make me fight you. Come on, deep down you *want* to give it back to me. Because we're vengeance demons and it's the right thing to do."

Vengeance demons? What the heck was that? I thought this was the Earth plane, given all the human-made buildings.

I could feel two sides of Gamma, no, Anastasia, warring with each other.

Gabriella's right. Stealing is wrong.

Shut up. She's all talk because even though she's older and she's completed her schooling already, she's scared of me. Scared of what I'm willing to do. Why should I give it back if she's too weak to fight for it?

But—

Hush! Something's off. There's a presence here.

Anastasia scanned the sky. That connection I'd felt ever since I'd laid eyes on the dot that had represented her—it would seem that she could feel it too.

Maybe my astral projection could only last so long. Maybe it would only be maintained if the people I was observing were unaware of me. Whatever the reason, the moment Anastasia started sensing my presence, something changed.

My bejeweled pendant got hot again. But rather than having my spirit return to Dualsing, I became visible, my hands and feet starting to solidify.

Anastasia cast a glance my way, her eyes locking with mine. I couldn't say which one of us was more shocked.

As I gained substance, the pendant lifted itself up and started pulling me closer to Anastasia, towing me forward and down by the neck.

As the distance between Anastasia and me lessened, the air grew heavier until it became an almost physical wall, as hard to penetrate as a knife to a bowl of Arcadian molasses.

Then suddenly, it got easier. A lot easier. And I flew toward her with frightening velocity.

I was reminded of that time when Eldon brought me a set of magnets imported from Earth and enchanted them to behave like they were still on their home plane. Eldon had attached a string to each magnet and tried to force the ends of similar poles to come together. That proved to be a futile exercise, and as soon as Eldon released one magnet, it swung around and attracted its other end to the second magnet's opposite pole.

The same was happening here. One moment Anastasia

and I couldn't possibly get any closer to each other, the next we were on a rapid collision course as if we were opposite ends of two magnets.

Inches before we hit each other, everything stopped.

It was like that moment when someone was about to wake up from a deep sleep. They could either force themselves to get up or turn over on the bed and continue sleeping.

I woke up.

Only half-solidified, I stared at my body on the floor of the observatory, with a frantic Alina trying to revive me in vain. By some instinct, I allowed myself to float higher, past the dome.

The Mirage Palace was laid out before me in a backdrop of the Dualsingian night sky.

Which was lit up by half a dozen tall buildings.

It looked like I had brought Anastasia's plane to Dualsing.

The world of eternal fountains and fantastic creatures merged with blocks after blocks of glass structures and harsh lights. The result was a scene as unnatural as it was beautiful.

My instinct urged me to move higher still. There, on the Dualsingian snow-capped mountain, was Anastasia and her cousin. Instead of a building rooftop, they were now on a small landing on the mountain, with a cliff's edge no more than a few feet away from them. This far up, the Mirage Palace was the size of a wood stump.

I drew closer.

"What the hell is going on?" Gabriella shouted, the girls' previous quarrel apparently forgotten in the face of a common enemy. Gabriella concentrated, and the pearl-studded earrings she wore glowed bright and a pair of midnight blue scaled wings appeared at her back. "Let's gear up."

She looked back at Anastasia, who had the same style of earrings, but the jewelry remained non-glowing. "Shit, I forgot you're a Powerless."

A Powerless. Was that like an Inadequate in Dualsing? From the waves of annoyance and self-disgust coming off Anastasia, I would bet the answer was yes.

As that annoyance and self-disgust turned into bitterness, I was glad that she no longer seemed able to see me, though I was only hovering a few feet above her. Maybe the change of environment was affecting her ability to sense me. At least for now.

The shrill cry of a bird of prey pierced the night, and the firefly-eagle swooped down on the girls, trying to knock them down as he did earlier with the hapless mountain goat, its bright body illuminating its entire course of attack.

Gabriella started mumbling spells under her breath, but she soon found the battle to be more of a physical one. The landing on which she stood was composed of a smooth, granite-like material, and drifting snow was accumulating on it. She fell twice mid-spell, barely avoided skidding off the landing as the firefly-eagle swept by.

Anastasia fared better. Though non-magical, or maybe because of it, her physique was superior to that of her cousin. She darted, rolled, hid between small rocks on the landing, anything to evade the firefly-eagle's touch down. Her agility was quite impressive, a smooth, graceful combination of martial arts, dance, and gymnastics.

After a few more attempts to knock the girls over the cliff with its weight, the firefly-eagle, with a wingspan twice as wide as my arms when fully stretched, seemed to have decided to change its strategy. It plunged down toward Anastasia like an arrow. Its sharp talons aimed straight for its intended victim's throat, its body a streak of bright light across the night sky.

"No!" I screamed, then realized I didn't have enough substance to produce the sound.

With her body crouched low, Anastasia growled and took out a wooden knife with lightning speed, driving it at the soft flesh on the ball of the firefly-eagle's right foot. At the last minute, the animal pulled up, barely making contact with the dull blade.

"What the hell are you doing? Use my dagger!" Gabriella yelled, not taking her eyes off their attacker.

After a small hesitation, Anastasia put away the wooden knife and took the dagger from her waist, but not before making sure that her hands were still fully gloved.

That action, plus the trepidation I could sense from her, made me realize that the girl was afraid of the dagger.

Afraid of iron.

I had no idea what it meant, since I didn't know enough about vengeance demons to know if a fear of iron was natural.

Another cry from the firefly-eagle drew Anastasia's eyes upward, searching the sky. She held the iron dagger with both of her hands. The enormous bird did another sweep of the sky before plunging faster and more menacingly than last time, its talons aimed at Anastasia's throat again.

Anastasia's grip on the dagger tightened while Gabriella got ready to pounce.

At the last possible moment, the bird pulled its lower body up and took off, missing the blade of the dagger by a mere inch. Then on its way up, its beak caught a corner of Anastasia's cloak. With powerful wings, it started dragging the girl off the small landing and to certain death in the deep valley below.

Anastasia lost her footing. Frantic, she dropped the dagger and tried to grab onto the rock at the edge of the landing, desperate to scramble back up the ledge. But with her hands gloved and her legs flailing in midair, it was only a matter of time before it was all over.

The firefly-eagle released the corner of Anastasia's cloak and took off, confident that its meal would be served upon its return.

"Take my hand!" Gabriella crouched down by the edge where Anastasia was hanging by a thread.

Anastasia took Gabriella's hand and moved her body side to side to create the momentum needed to swing herself back onto the landing.

But it didn't look like there would be enough momentum to do so. Exceptional physique or not, her arms could only support her body weight for so long.

Her hand started to slips from Gabriella's.

With a determined glint in her eyes, Anastasia swung back one last time, then leaned into the forward motion with everything she had.

Her movement started to slow right before her left foot reached the edge of the landing. She wasn't going to make it.

Then to my horror, she yanked on Gabriella's hand, using that extra bit of traction and opposite force to flip herself onto the landing even as Gabriella went over it.

Anastasia touched the ground with both of her feet like a cat, and then there was an awful silence before Gabriella hit the bottom of the cliff with a *thump*.

What was more chilling was the torrent of Anastasia's thoughts that assaulted me, all of them self-justifying.

It was her or me.

She found out I took the dagger.

It was only a matter of time before she figured out I was scared of iron.

It's her own fault for not thinking to use her magic to save me. I had to do whatever it took to save myself.

Blame evolution for her wings being vestigial. Great as a power indicator but totally useless for actual flying.

My pendent started shaking, almost as if it was overloaded by either Anastasia's cold-bloodedness or my terror, or a combination of both.

Anastasia looked up, seemingly drawn by the vibration of the pendent—or maybe it was that whatever connection was between us, she was now able to sense it again.

When she locked eyes with me for the second time tonight, I was convinced that my earlier theory was right, and that my invisibility would only be maintained if she was unaware of me. That was because the longer she glared at me, the more substantial I felt.

Her lips formed a cruel line as I came crashing down onto the landing.

Kill the witness, whoever the hell she is. She's most likely responsible for this blasted reality I'm in anyway.

Anastasia advanced toward me, pulling out the wooden knife. It might not be sharp, but in the hand of someone intending to do harm, it could still be lethal.

Then I saw it.

The iron dagger, left abandoned on the ground.

I was mesmerized by the gleaming metal I'd been taught

all my life to fear. But there was no fear now.

I picked up the dagger and faced Anastasia. There was no pain at the touch of the metal. No instant death as common sense dictated.

Who's Anastasia, a vengeance demon who's afraid of iron? Who am I, a fae who's not?

Seven

Eldon

"They took her."

I barged into the observatory with Trust by my side and found it empty except for a young pixie. She sat atop a large book, looking dejected.

"It's Alina, right?" I tried to keep the impatience out of my voice. One would always get more information out of others when a proper name was used, and I needed that because while Trust could sense it when Finny was in trouble, he wasn't entirely strong on the specifics. "Finny's told me so much about you."

The pixie bowed. "Your Royal Highness."

"What happened?"

Alina looked like she was ready to burst into tears. "We were working when she fainted. I found Mr. Lichen. He called the Centaur Guard and they took her away."

The Centaur Guard, the queen's private bodyguards. Now I knew Finny was *really* in trouble. The guards would be able to sense the residual signature of vengeance power in the air. Every type of magic left behind a distinct flavor, and vengeance magic was unmistakably bitter on the taste buds, like strong black tea.

"And oh, one more thing," Alina stopped me as I started

to leave. "Her pendant got really hot."

I spun around. "She was wearing that blasted pendant?"

"Yes. And it got hot."

Damn.

It had taken me years of patience and planning to get to this point, but all the preparation in the world could not have allowed me to anticipate this development.

The Eye of Sebille served as an indicator and enforcer of the Crossover. On Finny's birthday, it would transport her home, while returning the fae who took her place on the Vengeance plane back to Dualsing.

The Eye wasn't supposed to grow hot until a day or so before Finny's birthday, but it was standard procedure to place the pendant on someone like her early, just in case.

And now its premature activation was going to derail everything. I had to act quickly.

And that meant seeing my parents.

The south wing housed the royal residence of the king and queen. It had been a long time since I had been in their chambers. Seeing and interacting with them at official palace functions? Yes. Attending meetings and making decisions together with the rest of the ruling class? Yes. Having direct, private conversations? No.

Not since the day I'd turned sixteen and had *that* conversation with them.

Sometimes I wondered if it would've been kinder if the Age of Insight had been eighteen instead, and I found out the truth about Finny at the same time I had to say goodbye to her.

Instead, every Dualsingian teenager went through the uncomfortable years between sixteen and eighteen, when they knew who amongst them was not really a fae, yet they weren't allowed to reveal it to the victims in question.

They called it character building.

I called it the systematic nurturing of life-long apathy.

On the way to the south wing, I found a secluded corner and gestured for Trust to join me there. After placing an anti-eavesdropping spell over us to ensure privacy, I got right to the point. "You know what I must ask of you."

Trust nodded with solemn eyes.

"The wall of the royal chamber is embedded with blood-rubies, not Molten Amber. We won't have access to our scouts to know what to expect."

Trust nodded again, the determination in his eyes unwavering.

We continued our journey to the south wing. The dragon, long past his flame-breathing days, swaggered rather than flew toward our destination. His untrimmed claws made *click-click* sounds on the marble floor as we passed through the crowd at central square, went through a series of interconnecting hallways, and came to a stop in front of a heavy double door carved straight from a pair of thousand-year-old oak trees. Two centaurs with shiny manes and well-groomed tails stood guard.

Trust went on ahead, advancing on the guards and letting out a huff of air that would typically have been intimidating. In keeping with his ruse, however, not even a tiny cloud of white smoke came from his flaring nostrils. The guards ran their appraising eyes over the dragon's small body, noted with raised eyebrows the state of his scales, discolored from age and dull from a lack of regular polishing.

They ignored Trust, just as I had hoped. There was a great power in being underestimated. It would allow Trust to accompany me inside to visit the queen as a harmless pet rather than a cunning intellect, despite the fact that they should've known better. Trust was the longest-serving royal advisor in Dualsingian history before his forced retirement.

I coughed and stepped forward, noting that the guards seemed only slightly more impressed at the sight of me.

Good.

"I would like to request an audience with the king and queen." I used the sternest tone I could manage, one I practiced daily with a voice recorder, a human gadget I had smuggled into Dualsing through a planeswalker demon always ready for a quick profit.

The guards remained silent. From the vacant look taking over their eyes, I could tell that they were telepathically checking with the queen. After a moment they bowed, touched the doorknobs, and stood aside as the double doors swung open a lot faster than their weight should've allowed.

I crossed the threshold with Trust, noting how shallow the guards' bows were. Nothing new there.

What was new was the receiving area of the royal chamber. The room had always been elegantly decorated, but now beside priceless paintings and antique furniture, there was a brick fireplace in the corner that radiated flames but not heat, and a cream colored fur rug draped tastefully over a plush stool. A trio of pixies hovered by the crown molding, sprinkling the air with miniature snowflakes that disappeared as soon as they touched the ground without leaving a trace of watermark.

"Do you find it to your liking?" Queen Dulcina asked as she entered, though it was clear she wasn't really asking for approval. She wore a gown of vibrant green silk, her blond hair pinned in an elaborate bun heavy with pearls and eternal flowers. Her blue eyes were devoid of warmth, but as she glanced up at the falling snowflakes, there was a flicker of tenderness there.

Tenderness, but not for me.

I bowed. "Your Majesty." She let me kiss her hand.

"Your Highness," she replied.

I looked around, taking in the winter theme of the room. "You're getting ready."

"Yes, I am," she murmured as she dismissed the pixies with a wave of her hand. They were gone in a flash, taking their baskets of snowflakes with them. "I heard winters on the vengeance plane are a lot colder than here. I want Deirdre to have a good transition."

Deirdre, my twin sister, intended heir to the throne and apple of my mother's eye. I didn't want to talk about her, but the queen had Finny, and I couldn't afford to *not* play along.

"At least she didn't get assigned to the dimension that's parallel to the vengeance plane. Can you imagine her amongst humans?" I said. "Speaking of transition—"

"You're here for Lady Serafina, aren't you? You heard, I assume."

My surprise at her cutting to the chase must've shown on my face, for she laughed softly and gestured to the plush stool. "I'm keeping her under observation. It's for her own good. Sit down, my son. Your father and I have much to discuss with you."

And by that, she meant *she* had something to discuss

with me. When Dualsingians spoke of the king and queen, they really meant just the queen. The real ruler of Dualsing was Queen Dulcina. The king had so little power, even his name was forgotten from disuse. There was true power in a name, and without one, a fae, no matter who he or she was, would eventually fade from existence, like my father.

That was what was expected of me, in time.

Over my dead still-got-a-name body.

I sat, careful to follow the queen's command right away. My best weapon right now was to be underestimated, and in a perverse way, obedience held great power. My limp leg protested the sudden change of position, but I ignored it. "What would you like to discuss, Mother?"

Queen Dulcina walked to me, giving me no choice but to look up at her. "You have feelings for Lady Serafina. Not that it matters."

Of course not. My feelings for Finny were of no importance to the queen. Feelings only mattered if those they belonged to mattered.

I waited, not giving in to the temptation to say something to break the silence. Years of palace politics and well-practiced self-control had taught me when to use silence as a weapon.

"What *does* matter," the queen continued after a time. "Is the Trip. People are starting to talk."

The Trip, an adventure that awaited every fae in our world at the entrance to adulthood. Traveling to other planes after that point in our lives was strictly prohibited, as our bodies just weren't meant for multiple cross-dimensional travels. People always came to us, willingly or otherwise, not the other way around.

"I plan to go in a few months, I just got too busy with—"

I began giving the same old excuse.

"Your eighteenth birthday was almost a year ago. This delay is unprecedented."

I remained silent.

"There are nasty rumors abounding that say you're too weak to take on the Trip." Queen Dulcina glanced pointedly at my leg. "Do you understand how...unseemly this all looks?"

The queen wasn't concerned about her son's actual capability to complete the Trip, but only the undermining of the royal family's image if he didn't go.

"I *am* going," I insisted.

"Yes, you are. At first light tomorrow. I already commissioned the planeswalker demon to take you."

"And if I refuse?" I already knew the answer.

"On top of moving her schedule up, I'll see to it that we drain every bit of vengeance magic out of that girl before we dump her back on her real family's doorstep. The process will drive her insane, but that's not my concern," the queen said without batting an eye.

She planned to do that anyway, if it wasn't done already. The parasitic nature of a Dualsingian demanded that she not pass up such a delicious energy meal. It was one thing when Finny's power was untapped and hard to harvest, it was another when it was awakened and ripe for the picking.

"Have a good Trip. The Crossover will be over when you come back," Queen Dulcina said almost gently as she turned to leave the room. "And tell the pixies to make the snowflakes bigger."

"Mother." I hadn't called her that for a long time. "Can I ask you for one favor?"

"What is it?"

"Can I see her? One last time? Please?" I pleaded.

The queen hesitated, then seemed to make up her mind, "Come with me."

She took me and Trust to a small study off the main receiving area. In the middle of it was a small bed. She pulled back the drapes and there was Finny, in an unnatural state that was neither sleep nor unconsciousness. She looked like she was in stasis, yet vengeance magic radiated from her as strongly as when she had yelled at me on the battlement.

I looked at the queen and she shrugged. "She's been like this since my guards found her at the observatory."

The Eye of Sebille vibrated, and together with Finny, started to fade. The embroidery adorning her lace pillow, mostly blocked by her head just moments ago, became visible.

"What is happening?" The queen pulled on my arm. "Why is Serafina disappearing? We have to get her back or Deirdre will be lost too!"

Of course. Everything was always about her precious Deirdre. The Eye of Sebille was as responsible for sending Finny packing as it was for bringing my sister home.

All right, Finny fading wasn't part of the plan, but it was time to improvise.

I turned to Trust. "Please reveal yourself."

EIGHT

Serafina

ANASTASIA NARROWED HER EYES ON the iron dagger in my hand. "Don't be stupid. I can take that from you in half a second."

I looked down at the valley where Gabriella had fallen to her death and swallowed. I was painfully aware that the landing was too slippery and small for a lot of maneuvering, and my potential killer outmatched me in both combat skills and ruthlessness, not to mention having the help of a wooden knife. And yet...

"Then why don't you?" I had no idea what gave me the courage to dare her. Maybe it was a matter of having nothing to lose.

"You don't think I can?" Anastasia's voice was full of arrogance and contempt, but inside her head, an entirely different conversation was taking place.

Don't touch the dagger! My gloves are torn.

Her scent. There's something there. She has power.

Vengeance power.

But how? She looks about my age but her power is totally raw and untrained.

Don't make a move until there's more information.

Rather than looking at Anastasia's cold and calculating

face, I focused on her pearl-studded earrings. They looked like any ordinary, non-magical trinkets. Non-glowing. I remembered how Gabriella seemed to be able to draw power from hers by energizing them, and how she'd called Anastasia a Powerless.

Anastasia's earrings must have been dormant because she wasn't able to activate them.

If they wouldn't glow bright for Anastasia, would they do so for me? The pearls pulled at me, making me believe that I could, even though I wasn't wearing them and I wasn't their owner.

How did Gabriella do it? She'd concentrated her thoughts on something and it had just happened.

What did I usually think about before my power manifested itself?

Justice.

Could justice also be the source of Gabriella's power, and thus the key to command the pearls? I'd never even heard of vengeance demons before this day, but it made sense given their name. Vengeance. Right and Wrong. Justice.

"What are you staring at?" Anastasia snapped. "Look me in the eye, dammit!"

Feeling silly, especially in light of Anastasia's hostility, I started counting out her sins in my head.

The wrongness of stealing another's dagger.

The wrongness of pushing someone to their death.

The wrongness of doing so when they were trying to help you.

Anastasia's earrings lit up our dark surrounding.

"What did you do?" She demanded sharply, turning her head left and right to confirm that it was indeed her earrings that were illuminating the area.

"And what is *that*?" She pointed at something behind me.

I twisted my body around, catching the edge of a wing. I twisted the other way and saw another. In awe, I realized that there was a pair of half transparent wings attached to my back.

They were a part of me.

As I was a part of the vengeance demon race.

That was my last thought before Anastasia lunged toward me.

Nine

Eldon

THE DRAGON WALKED A FEW steps away from me and started shaking his body like a wet puppy. With each shake, the surface of his scales looked more polished, frayed edges became smooth, and small bald patches on his body disappeared. His eyes, crowded with cataracts just moments before, became clear and shrewd.

With a roar, the miniature dragon shed the last of his glamour, letting go of his age-beaten illusion. He revealed himself as a vivacious beast in all his magnificent glory, a shimmer of gold surrounded his full wings, reflective of his deep reservoir of ancient magic.

"What manner of trickery is this?" the queen demanded. She tried to call her fae magic to contain Trust, but he blew a huff of white smoke on her and rendered her frozen to her spot.

"This should hold her for a while," Trust said in a satisfied voice that suggested he'd wanted to do that for a long time.

The dragon, millennia old, was once the trusted advisor to generations of Dualsing kings and queens. As time passed, however, the Dualsingian rulers listened less and less to the old dragon, considering his ideas outdated, his voice unimportant. So he became that which he was believed to be—old and mute. Just as the current king had lost his name after being considered unworthy of mention. In our world, perception altered reality.

Trust had stayed that way for centuries, moping around the palace, too big to be overlooked as a pixie would be, and too aesthetically imperfect to be accepted by the beauty-conscious unicorns. That was the way he had been when I'd first met him as a child. Even at that age, I was drawn to unfortunate creatures such as him.

I treated him like a playmate and passed onto him trinkets gifted by visiting royals. Even pretty things given out of politeness to a not-so-favored crown prince were more than what the neglected draconic ex-statesman had received in a very long time.

And dragons did love their trinkets.

In return, he became my confidant and most loyal supporter. Through my acknowledgement of his existence, Trust regained his voice and health, though he was careful to maintain the illusion of his former state of being. He told me one should always have an element of surprise.

I turned back to the bed, and found Finny had completely vanished, not even an outline of her was left.

"We have to act now," I said.

"Are you sure?" Trust approached me, speaking in a deep, grave voice. "The risk was high enough before, but now..."

"It would be no worse than if we never tried."

My original plan was to harvest enough magic through the Molten Amber—their strength was knowledge and knowledge was power—to fuel Trust's ancient spell and make everyone forget about Finny being an outsider. With all the pre-Crossover political song and dance happening around the palace, I had almost stored up enough magic to do exactly that. But now the priority was to get Finny back.

"'No worse than if we never tried'? Dear boy, there are always worse things than inaction."

"We have to act now. We don't have a choice," I pointed at the bed. "She's gone. She could be anywhere across the planes right now."

It seemed to be the last point regarding Finny that finally convinced Trust. Finny had been by my side when the dragon first came into my life. Though Trust had chosen to reveal his true self only to me, there was no doubt he was fond of the kind-hearted Finny.

"All right then. Do you have what I need?"

I took a flame-red hair charm out of my pants pocket. I'd taken it from the observatory before heading here, despite the protests of little Alina. I undid the charm and smoothened out the hair strand. "Here's one."

I walked to the bed, ran my hand over the lace pillow, hating myself for hoping that the Centaur Guard wasn't entirely gentle when handling Finny. There, a small piece of brown hair, no doubt pulled out as they settled her on the bed and rearranged her braid. "Here's the other one."

Placing the two strands side by side on the dragon's palm, the hairs drew close to each other like magnets, reflecting the intertwined fates, or maybe even the closeness of the physical locations of their owners.

"This should do it. I should be able to call Lady Serafina back through her pendant."

Trust started chanting an incantation in a long-forgotten language. The two strands of hair started to fall away, then wrapped around each other in a bid to form a dead knot.

"What's happening?" I asked Trust.

"It can't be," the dragon breathed. "My spell caught both Lady Serafina and your sister right in the middle of some kind of cross-dimensional merge, during a battle for life. My magic has intensified their connection rather than disengaging it."

"Dammit. And what do you mean, a battle for life?" What had we done? Merged realities between two connected individuals were extremely rare occurrences. For us to attempt a rescue right when the merge was happening was pure rotten luck. It was almost enough for me to start worshipping the long-abandoned Fates. "Can you unwind them?"

"Yes, but—"

"Do it!"

TEN

Serafina

ONE MOMENT ANASTASIA'S WOODEN KNIFE was seconds from making contact with my belly, the next the merged world we'd shared unraveled itself.

Her wooden knife hit a barrier. On her side, there was the rooftop and a city of glass structures and a million lights. On my side, there was the dark sky and the landing and the snow-capped mountain.

Then her side winked out of existence, leaving me in Dualsing and Dualsing only, my wings retracted and my body remained solid.

And uninjured.

I barely had time to let out a breath of relief before I started falling down the mountain, being pulled backward by my pendant. My body yanked through space, my scream lost in flight.

It was over before I truly had a chance to become frightened. I expected to land back on the floor of the observatory, with the anxious face of Alina above me. Instead, I found my feet solidly planted in the central square of the palace, with its exotic jade-crowned crane and ivory columns.

I tightened my left fist and was pleased and surprised to

find the iron dagger still within its grasp. With everything that was happening, I'd forgotten all about it. I touched my pendant. It was there too, cool to the touch now.

A fine mist covered the entire square, and everything was silent, which was unusual for the bustling square.

That was because everything was frozen.

I could see pixies and the jade-crowned crane in mid-flight, the water droplets from the eternal fountain sparkling in the sun like perfectly round, stationary pearls. Far away, on a balcony of the east wing, a servant was beating a rug, except the rug was at a forty-five degree angle with the ground and unmoving. So was the woman holding the stick.

What was going on? The merged realities had resolved themselves. Everything should've gone back to normal.

"I really made a mess of it, didn't I?" came Eldon's voice from behind me.

I dropped the knife and it clattered loudly against the cobblestones. When I turned, I found Eldon standing by a potted cherry tree, his miniature dragon at his side.

"What's going on?" I voiced the same question I had asked just hours earlier; it felt like a lifetime ago. "And why aren't you and Trust frozen like the others?"

Then I took a closer look at Trust and did a double take. The dragon looked like those described in children's history books—its wings wrapped in a gold lining, its scales glossy and vibrant.

A champion worthy of a king.

Eldon drew close until he was looking me in the eyes. "Trust made it all happen. I asked him to. Then I asked him to bring you here."

My jaw fell open. I always knew that Trust was more

intelligent than everyone gave him credit for, but if he was somehow responsible for the stasis that seemed to be enveloping the palace, then it would suggest some advanced spell-casting abilities as well.

Just as the children's history books described.

"I'll let you explain," Trust nodded to Eldon and retreated. I never even knew that the dragon could talk. How many more surprises could I take?

"Eldon?" I whispered. I was a little afraid of the answer now.

"I did it for us. So that we can be together."

"What are you talking about?"

"Trust is a powerful ancient, and he's been trying to help me for a long time now. Please, let me explain everything from the very beginning. It's the only way any of this is going to make sense."

I let out a shaky breath. "All right."

"Do you know what Dualsing is really built on?"

"What do you mean?"

"I mean its economy. I know that fae hate talking about earthly matters such as wealth and finances, but do you ever wonder how the plane supports itself?"

"I know there's some sort of trade going on. The palace always has traders visiting from other planes." I licked my suddenly dry lips. "But what does that have to do with anything?"

"It has to do with everything." Eldon laughed bitterly. "In every generation, Dualsingians choose a selection of their younglings, put glamours on them, and switch them with children in other races with the help of the planeswalker demons. They chose host families of highborn status, with old magic who would raise the Dualsingians as their own and divulge their ancient secrets to them. The glamour will make sure they see the children as their own, though somewhat defective because obviously the glamour could not actually fake magical powers. Then at the age of eighteen, these children are welcomed home as heroes and spend the rest of their days selling what they've learned through a long-established network of black-markets. Spells. Military strategies. Secret codes. Even closely guarded wine recipes. You name it, we sell it."

"That's...that's despicable." The bile from my stomach rose. "So all those royal visitors..."

"...are really black marketeers. Each more shady than the next. Information is the most powerful commodity and it fetches a high price."

"But why support yourself this way? There are more honest ways to make a living."

"Why do cuckoos and cowbirds lay their eggs in others' nests to be raised as their own? It is the way of my people. The other planes called us the Changelings, and we'd been hated through all the ages for what we do as a race. In our generation, there's a good number who have been sent out there."

"All those patterns I saw on the dome—"

"Eglantina-Six, Marigold-Twelve, Oda-whatever. Of course these are not their real names, but they're all planes whose inhabitants are unknowingly caring for Changelings children right at this moment. It is Mr. Lichen's job to oversee the progress of these children."

"Like Alpha, Beta, and—"

"Gamma, the only Changeling of royal blood. My twin sister.

"Twin sister." I rolled the two words around on my

tongue. I'd never heard of Eldon having a sister, let alone a twin. And did Eldon just mention the return happening at the age of eighteen? Suddenly I knew where this conversation was heading. I tried to back away, but Eldon took my hands in his.

"Finny, my sister was sent to the vengeance plane, and the baby she was switched with was—"

"—me," I mouthed soundlessly. "So I *am* a vengeance demon."

"It was considered a great accomplishment getting her into such a predominant family. As you can imagine, it's not easy pulling the wool over a vengeance demon's eyes." The corner of Eldon's lips twisted. "Her return will be widely celebrated, and a real shakeup of the political landscape."

I was right. I really was connected with Anastasia— because she'd taken my place with my real parents. A part of me was in utter shock, yet the other part wasn't surprised at all. I always knew Dualsing wasn't my real home.

"Trust told me you were in that merged reality with her. You figured out who you are when you were in there, didn't you?"

"Yes. But that means I'm really a demon." I could almost be all right with the vengeance part, but being a demon sounded rather evil and terrifying. I pulled my hands back and rubbed them. They were ice cold.

Eldon quickly added, "Demons are not as bad as they're depicted in our world. And vengeance demons are the most respected of them all. It is Dualsingians who are seen as scum by the rest of the Cosmic Balance. That's why our location is hidden and untraceable through all magical means."

"No wonder Lord and Lady Sebille never accepted me." I bit down on my lips until I tasted blood. Tears threatened to fill my eyes. "My entire life. Everything. I'm nothing but a means of making a profit for them."

"Not their profit. The queen's. That only made the Sebilles more resentful of you. The queen should've been the one who took you in, according to tradition. But she couldn't bear the sight of you, because you reminded her of what she'd lost."

"And you knew about this?" All the time we spent on the battlement. All the times I had shared with him my longing for my parents' love and my puzzlement over their aloofness. I was nothing more than the main attraction for the Crossover, and he hadn't said a single word. He'd let me waste countless hours wondering why I was so different and so unloved.

"Everyone knows. Once they turn sixteen," Eldon said softly. "I'm sorry I couldn't tell you sooner. Your pendant creates the portal for the Crossover, and it could be triggered pre-maturely if you have knowledge of what's to come. I didn't want to lose you."

I didn't want to hear that. Not now when all my emotions were in upheaval. So I concentrated on the next piece of the puzzle I could think of. "The Eye of Sebille, that's not really a jewel of the Sebille house, is it?"

"No. It's the eye of whatever house happened to be hosting someone like you through the ages."

"People like me. Through the ages. I can't imagine their real families, *my* real family, being too happy about the kidnapping."

"That's why they sent you to work with Mr. Lichen.

Getting you trained with him is their one and only gift to you. The Reveal is essentially a Dualsingian tracking and anti-concealment ability. In their warped minds, their debt to you is paid in full with that imparted knowledge. That, and the fact that they allowed you to keep your true name all this time."

"So my name is really Serafina." At least there was one constant in my life. I liked my name. And I'd been Serafina my entire life—I couldn't imagine being called anything else.

"Yes, Serafina Anastasia Advocatus. There's power in having a real name that's regularly used."

"Anastasia." So my replacement in the vengeance world had taken on my middle name. I wondered if she'd done it because deep down she knew Serafina wasn't her true name.

I was no fae. Everything I'd been taught was false. It was too much to take in. Then something occurred to me.

"Wait, then your twin sister is—"

"—the true heir to the throne." Eldon's lips curled. "Crown Princess Deirdre of Dualsing. Guess they should've reserved the code name Alpha for her, huh? Officially, the reason for me not being chosen for the switch was because of my leg. The truth is, my mother loved Deirdre at first sight. There is no logic to it. It simply is. She wanted her daughter to have the crown, and all the vengeance secrets Deirdre is bringing back will cement that position. I can't compete with that. Even if I was whole."

Something about his words chilled me to the bone. He saw Deirdre as competition, not kin.

I narrowed my eyes and took another look at our surroundings. I knew him well enough to know when he wasn't telling me something important. If I hadn't been so shocked over everything, I would've question it a lot sooner. "Eldon, what have you done? What did you ask Trust to do?"

"A forgetting spell that covers all of Dualsing. It's going to make every man and woman forget that you're not one of us."

That way, I could go on living here, with everyone around me not remembering that they were supposed to shun me, that I was a temporary annoyance to be put up with for merely eighteen years. I would be accepted, maybe even loved in time...

One look at a nearby pixie, eerily still in her mid-somersault, shook me like a bucket of cold water. Her eyes, staring into nothing, reminded me that what Eldon proposed wasn't natural.

"Why is everyone frozen?"

"That's the part that I messed up. The spell is supposed to be instantaneous. I never knew that your connection with my sister would become so strong. To sever it and make everyone forget her, the spell needed more time to run its course. They should unfreeze very shortly. After that, the only ones who will know your true origin will be you, me, and Trust."

I got what Eldon wasn't telling me. For the spell to be taking this long to take effect, it meant it wasn't all that stable, and he was risking the well-being of all those who got caught in it. "You sure the spell is meant to hold?"

"It'll hold. It has to," Eldon insisted.

"And the pendant?" I touched it again. It remained cool to the touch.

"A second spell. It's going to take away the pendant's ability to trigger the Crossover."

"Closing the connection to Deirdre, making sure she can never return?" The girl might've tried to kill me, but it was still a rotten thing to do, denying her the chance to know her real legacy and condemning her to a lifetime of feeling like she doesn't belong. I knew how that felt.

"She'll never know. She'll simply never be claimed by Dualsing. She'll live and die thinking she's a vengeance demon."

"Yes, but one without any vengeance magic." I couldn't believe the Eldon I knew could be so heartless regarding his own sibling.

"Think about us, Finny," Eldon urged. "This way you and I can stay together. Listen, you don't understand. Remember I told you Dualsing's location is a well-guarded secret? That means if you leave, you'll never be able to find your way back here. I'll lose you forever."

Never finding my way back to the only home I'd ever known. Never seeing the boy I'd cared for my whole life ever again. Yet, no matter how I looked at it, it was the only way.

"I know. But you have to stop this. I can't, in good conscience, allow you to do this." Damn my vengeance demon instincts—showing me the just thing to do even if it was killing me.

"What about us?" Eldon gritted his teeth.

I was prepared to say goodbye to him at the battlement because of the lies between us. Now I had to do the same for the sake of the truth staring me in the face.

"Answer me honestly. How much of this is you wanting me, and how much of this is you wanting the crown?" I would give anything to hear him say he did it all just to be with me, but I knew him too well to fool myself.

"Can't I want both? Can't I have both?" he retorted. "Why can't we both win for once in our lives?" Eldon banged his fist on a nearby marble table, cracking it.

"Because it's not right." I stood straighter. A sense of calm came over me amongst the sadness. "You've wanted that crown since we were toddlers. You've wanted it so badly that everything else comes second. A part of you is still that child, desperately wanting to be loved. You want it all and you want it for all the wrong reasons. I will not be your tool. I will not be a part of this deception. Reverse the spell, Eldon, before anyone realizes what you're attempting. Before the stasis destabilizes. We'll let nature take its course."

"You're going to go through with the celebration, knowing the high point is them dumping you back at your real family's doorstep? A family and a world you know nothing about?" Eldon rubbed his hands over his face.

"Yes." I refused to let him see how this was breaking my heart. One sign of weakness, and he would never let me go. I knew enough about these spells to know that without my willing consent to be a part of it, the false reality would fall apart. My will was my only bargaining chip, but by everything that was sacred to me, was I tempted to say yes.

I knew the exact moment he accepted defeat. It was in the way his shoulders sagged and his eyes grew tired as he sighed.

"Very well. I'll ask Trust to call it off," he said softly.

"Thank you." They were such ironic words to utter, but I knew not what else to say.

"You insist on doing this, even after Princess Deirdre tried to kill you in the merged reality?" Trust asked me, appearing by Eldon's side.

I nodded.

"Kill? What are you talking about?" Eldon asked sharply. "You didn't tell me she was trying to kill Finny."

The dragon turned to Eldon. "That's not the only thing I lied to you about. All these years, I have had a hidden agenda in helping you."

"What are you talking about?" The look of betrayal on Eldon's face pulled at me. Trust was one of the only beings Eldon had allowed into his life. First me choosing justice over him, now this.

"In my long years, I've studied the stars. Your sister is foretold to be one of the most terrifying queens in Dualsingian history. I thought by helping you gain the throne, I could prevent many tragedies from happening. I didn't count on Lady Serafina's integrity." The dragon shook his head, his soft beard swaying with the motion. "Maybe I wasn't meant to stop it."

Trust started fading away. "I'll leave you two be. The spell will be broken soon. When it is, everyone will lose the memory of the last day, except the three of us. Take care to hide your power until the Crossover, m'lady, or they *will* try to extract it from you."

I thanked him for the warning.

After Trust was gone, Eldon took out a handkerchief and bent down to retrieve the iron dagger I'd dropped. Carefully, he put the wrapped knife in his vest pocket, in a tentativeness that mirrored his twin sister's when she too had to handle the blade.

I looked at him questioningly.

"I won't lie and say I'm taking this to avoid people raising alarm when they find it. I'm taking it because it was yours, and I want something to remember you by."

"But it's not mine—" I started to correct him.

"I don't care. The blade was no more yours than you were mine." He touched my cheek. "It's apt, isn't it?"

I closed my eyes to keep from weakening my resolve at the sorrow in his eyes. Or maybe I just didn't want him to see the same emotions reflected in my own. But his next words had me opening them wide.

"I might as well take the Trip at first light as the queen has commanded, even though she won't remember commanding it. I couldn't stand the next two weeks, seeing you and knowing you're already lost to me."

I disagreed. I would rather have another two weeks of being with him, memorizing his beloved face, every stolen moment, even if it would only serve to mock what I would never have.

I wrapped my arms around Eldon and kissed him. He kissed me back, holding me tight.

When we finally broke apart and I tasted salt on my lips, I wasn't sure if the tears were mine or Eldon's.

"As a prince of Dualsing, I'm giving you two boons," he whispered in my ear. "One. You can call on me for help. All you have to do is say my name. Do not hesitate to call when you need it."

Once and once only. That was the unspoken part of the offer. After the Trip, every Dualsingian had in them the tolerance for only one more cross-dimensional round trip. I knew then that I would never call for his help, never say his name aloud ever again. As long as I never called, I would always have the hope to see him again. To look forward to that moment. Maybe I would do it when I was an old woman, so I could see him one last time right before I passed on.

"And what is the second boon?" I forced the words past the lump in my throat, all around us the world had started to unfreeze. The wings of a jade-crowned crane began to flip down, propelling its body to fly upward as surely as Eldon's exit from my life.

"I'll make sure that a switch will never be performed on your future children," Eldon said fiercely. "They will never go through what you went through. That's a promise."

Epilogue

Serafina

A Year Later...

"**B**EFORE EXACTING YOUR ASSIGNED VENGEANCE, reconnaissance within reason is allowed under Article 4.3, section E of the IICVD handbook..." Professor Mando continued to talk, but I couldn't take a single word in.

Clang...clang-clang-clang...clang-clang...

Madeleine Abrianna Lex tapped her heels on the stone floor in front of her seat at the lecture room at the University of Demonic Studies. The popular girl had embedded a pair of miniature horseshoes in her heels, and with each tap, she hammered out a wave of vibration. Judging from the smug smile she sent my way, she thought the vibration would be unnerving for me.

Everybody knew of my Dualsingian——no, Changeling——background. Madeleine probably figured that since I was raised by a people who feared iron, I would be conditioned to think in the same way. A new girl to a new way of life. Easy target.

There would always be bullies no matter what plane one was on.

It had been a year since I'd landed on the front lawn of

the Advocatus Mansion, my birth family's primary residence, and I'd found myself no more accepted on the vengeance plane than I was at Dualsing. The prominent Advocatus family, publicly humiliated by being fooled into raising a changeling and having a family member killed by her, was single-mindedly determined to act as if the switch had never happened. Unfortunately, that line of thinking had also bred the expectation that I ought to catch up on all things vengeance in a very short period of time. I barely spent two months with around-the-clock private tutors before being enrolled at the university, competing with peers who had spent their entire lives gaining the vengeance education.

Ironically, I'd simply traded parents who were indifferent with ones who cared too much for the wrong reasons.

The new confidence I gained when I first discovered my vengeance demon destiny eroded over time, the shock of adjusting to my new world had left me skittish and closed up. Worse, whenever I did vengeance practice sessions, I kept identifying my targets with Eldon, and found myself trying to help them rather than punish them.

If I couldn't get through to Eldon, if I couldn't afford to be soft in light of what he did, then maybe I could make it up by giving my targets a second chance.

The result was failing grades and even more sneers from my classmates.

I hugged myself tightly, feeling cold inside. I wasn't terrified by the onslaught of pulsation from Madeleine's heel; I was overwhelmed by the hardship of my transition that her action symbolized.

When would I be accepted? Would I ever be? I had been

thrown into a world of skyscrapers and systemic vengeance training, with a rightful place in an old and prestigious family, yet I had not made a single friend. Not even the pixies on this plane liked me, as they too despised the Dualsingians for making servants of their kind.

I faced animosity every day. I didn't know why it was hitting me especially hard today. But it was. Maybe the stress was accumulating and I'd just had enough of dirty looks, nasty whispers and outright intimidation.

Finny, are you all right?

I couldn't breathe. That was Eldon's voice in my head, soft and faint yet distinctively his.

Trust has allowed me to tune in to your mood. To make sure you're all right.

I was touched by his concern at the same time I was disturbed by having my mood monitored without my knowledge. What was that term the humans used— invasion of privacy?

Unfortunately the communication is not two-way, and I could only pick up the huge spikes. You're upset. A pause. *Maybe I should come to you.*

He hesitated because he was afraid of making the wrong call, knowing he only got one shot. Ever. If I didn't calm myself down right away, he would assume I was in serious trouble and come to this plane. If so, I'd never see him again after today.

Finny. More urgent now. *What is happening? You're even more agitated than a moment ago.* He must've picked up on my dismay at the thought of never laying eyes on him again. *Hang in there. I'm coming.*

There was more at stake than wasted chances. He would come and he would kill Madeleine. I knew that not only because he was protective of me, but because he had it in him.

He didn't show his own sister any mercy.

I might not like my arrogant classmate, but I didn't want her death on my conscience.

I took a breath, then released it slowly. I repeated, each breath more deliberate than the last, forcing my heart rate to decline. Projecting a mental picture of tranquility when I felt anything but was straining, and I folded my body in a near-fetal position on the classroom chair, my muscles shaking from the orchestrated effort.

The tapping from Madeleine's heel continued.

"Now, I'm going to pass around my own vengeance dagger for you to see. You youngsters will get yours when you graduate from this program. Notice the carving on the left side, which originated in the eleventh century..." I couldn't see the commemorative dagger Professor Mando was referring to from my angle, but I didn't have to. I knew it would be the same as the iron one Anastasia, or Deirdre, had stolen from Cousin Gabriella.

Ding.

"Ouch!" someone screamed.

The dagger hit the ground right after I felt a protective shield encompassed me, neutralizing my volatile bio-readings more effectively than mere deep breathing and controlled heart rate.

I knew the moment Eldon eased up. It wasn't what he said, but the impression of him being relieved.

It looks like whatever it was, it's resolved. A long pause. *Take care, Finny.*

Then he was gone, leaving me feeling relieved and disappointed at the same time.

I uncurled myself from my fetal position, looked up and around the class, dazed at the turn of events and wondering where that perfectly timed shield came from.

"Oops," Megan Aequitas, a vengeance demon and trickster hybrid, said with just a little too much regret in her voice. She glanced at me with mischievous eyes, and my gut told me the shield was sent by her.

"What's wrong, Miss Lex? Why did you scream?" Professor Mando frowned at Madeleine. Her scream hadn't even registered with me at the time, but now that I thought about it, I would bet that the dropped dagger had sent a resonating feedback straight to Madeleine's iron-centered heels, ricocheting through her head like a shrieking banshee.

"Nothing, sir. I was caught off guard by the sound of the drop, that's all." Madeleine smiled weakly at our lecturer, then gave Megan a look of pure hatred.

"Remember, a vengeance demon should never be so easily startled. It's our job to startle *them*."

The snobbish girl's face flushed, and Megan squared her shoulders. She'd stopped Madeleine's bullying, knowing there would be consequences.

Right then and there, I made up my mind to befriend Megan Aequitas. I was too wrapped up in my own misery and readjustment to connect with anyone before, but I was ready now.

THE END

Note from Louisa: Did you enjoy BEFORE VENGEANCE? If so, I would really appreciate it if you could write an Amazon and/or Goodreads review!

DISCOVER THE VENGEANCE WORLD SERAFINA WAS THROWN INTO

Megan is a typical university student trying to figure out her place in the world, except instead of hoping to pass the bar or get into med school, she's studying to become a licensed vengeance demon.

Nineteen-year-old Megan Aequitas is the only vengeance demon and trickster hybrid ever born. In a world where vengeance demons are respectable, rule-obsessed guardians of the Cosmic Balance, and tricksters are playful, happy-go-lucky perpetrators of chaos, being half and half is, well, tricky.

Determined to prove herself worthy of her vengeance blood, Megan enrolls in University of Demonic Studies' prestigious co-op program. Wreaking karmic revenge on wrongdoers from cheaters to crooks sounds fun and simple, if it weren't for the unsuspecting human roommate, Megan's flamboyant trickster half-brothers, a changeling-raised fellow outcast, and a trio of evil wannabes. Then one assignment turns deadly when Megan discovers a plot to unleash an ancient force so authoritarian, most creatures would be deemed too unworthy to exist.

After a lifetime of being embarrassed by her trickster tendencies and striving to fit in vengeance society, Megan now has to learn to embrace both of her worlds if she wants to save them.

EXCERPT
VENGEANCE BE MINE

T HERE IS A SAYING AMONGST vengeance demons—justice comes slowly, but surely.

Or on rare occasions, it could hit hard and fast, like the waves of contractions my male target was experiencing as I stood over him.

"Make it stop. I'm begging," he groaned, arching his back on the hotel bed. His T-shirt was drenched, like in those bar contests he frequented, revealing the long torso and lean six-pack of an athlete in his prime. He looked up at me, his brown eyes pleading, and his gaze unfocused—the way humans got when they were in pain.

"Mr. Lodge, it's not even midnight yet. We've got another four hours of torment to go, according to my work order." I tried to sound professional, but my nineteen-year-old voice was just a bit on the squeaky side, even to my own ears. The business of vengeance was harder than I'd ever thought possible.

This was my first solo practice session after a year of in-class lectures at the University of Demonic Studies, Faculty of Arts and Vengeance. I needed it to go well.

Problem was, none of my textbooks mentioned how to deal with a crybaby.

A crying *man*-baby.

MVP Jeremy Lodge, aka "The Machine," clutched his stomach and whimpered. The famous basketball star was known for striking fear in the hearts of opposing teams all over the world, but now the only thing that came knocking was another contraction.

"What's happening?" The Machine panted during a respite, the tranquility of the hotel room clearly lost on him. There was soft light from the paper lantern overhead and a fluffy sand-colored carpet one could sink one's toes into. The sliding doors made of mint-frosted glass added a touch of modern elegance to the five-star suite.

What was happening? What a question.

When I'd fantasized about getting my vengeance demon designation, this was the part I'd found the most satisfying—telling the target how his actions had led to the consequences he was facing.

"A taste of childbirth pain, which is a fitting punishment for cheating on your pregnant wife with the whole cheerleading squad."

I had to pat myself on the shoulder for coming up with *that* particular punishment. Why exact a boring old vengeance when you could spice it up with a cool, ironic twist?

"You little bitch!" The Machine pounded his enormous fist on the mattress.

"Hey, the name is Megan. Not bitch. Not little." I gritted my teeth.

"Fuck you!"

I pushed aside my first instinct—getting mad or, worse, scared. I'd been insulted before, but usually with more subtlety than that. I guess humans weren't exactly subtle creatures. It might also be the difference between having the cuss words tossed at me, rather than learning them in a classroom setting. I forced myself to unclench my fists, my fingernails peeled away from the imprints they dug into my palms almost reluctantly. There was a magical barrier between us, and I was in control.

Even though it was my first time alone with a target.

I straightened. Never show fear, they'd taught us in *Occupational Insults & Threats 101*. "Bad manners will only get me mad and extend your punishment."

"I'm going to kill you," he snarled.

"Alright, an extra ten minutes it is."

Was insisting on ten too harsh? Should I have said five? I caught myself brushing my fingertips over the edge of the pocket-sized training manual currently pressed against my jean-clad bum. This being my first time, I'd packed the mini-bible along just in case. Now I longed to take it out and flip to the chapter on *How to Deal With the Misgivings of Hurting In the Name of Justice*, because every single moan that came out of The Machine hit my guts like ice water. Since I wasn't the target's direct victim, it was hard for me to establish him as the total bad guy in my mind, and part of me felt bad about administrating the suffering to him. Green, green, green—that was what I was.

Come on, Megan. You can't afford a soft heart. You want to help people, remember? Keeping balance in the world is helping them.

I sometimes forgot how annoyingly logical my inner voice could be.

"I swear, I'm going to kill you," The Machine repeated, every muscle on his body taut, his eyes promising death and destruction. Had I been a mortal, I would have been scared shitless.

I sighed. "I heard you the first time. How about you try *not* cheating in the future?"

The Machine looked ready to explode into a string of curses when his eyes widened to the size of saucers.

Halftime was over, and there was no sitting this round out.

"Alright, listen up." I hastily leaned over. I had under a minute to get him to understand. "Breathe in through your nose and out through your mouth. In for three, then out for three. Come on, I've read these exercises on your Internet and it should help."

Oh boy, it was going to be a long night. At least the target was contained within a dome-shaped energy barrier covering the entire bed. An attack from over two hundred pounds of pure muscle was something I did not need.

And so the labor carried on past midnight. And on. And on.

According to my training manual, I was supposed to stay with the target throughout the entire process. I tried, I really did. But after three hours of his moaning and bitching, I'd had enough. Why, oh why, was my fickle magic able to mute the noise for all humans within hearing range, but not for me?

The grating sound of torment caused my head to pound with the intensity of a full-blown aura migraine, the queen of all migraines that even a supernatural being couldn't escape. First came the offending aura; a whirling circle of flashing light the size of a penny appeared in my visual field. Soon, it expanded to cover most of my vision, pretty much blinding me. When the aura dissipated, that was when the nausea, dizziness, and excruciating pain in my skull started. Fun.

I stumbled out of the bedroom and sank down on the sofa in the dim living room, my temples throbbing. There was still another hour of vengeance to go, but my magic should maintain his torment for a while in my absence. Right now, my priority was to survive until this terrible pain in my skull went away, and that meant putting some distance between The Machine and me.

It was two in the morning, and the floor-to-ceiling window greeted me with a view of the Toronto Harbor. Mercifully, the yachts pushed only feeble light into the surrounding darkness, and the undisturbed water calmed my nerves. I did mention I was sensitive to light in my current state, right?

I hoped it would get easier with each job, like Dad had claimed.

At long last my migraine subsided, but I wasn't ready to face the howling athlete just yet. I was still on the clock, and The Machine was still suffering. Who was there to see that I wasn't actually *in* the room the entire time? I just needed a few more minutes. It was more than fair, considering the occupational hazard.

As if on cue, The Machine's wails took on a kicked-in-the-balls tone, only to change pitch midway into a string of inventive swear words, most of which I'd never even heard before.

I turned on the lights, took out *Renters Weekly* from my backpack and sifted through the roommates-wanted ads. Now that the in-class segment of my demon education was almost over, bye-bye college dorm, hello sweet independence.

As I lost myself in the magazine, The Machine's yowls faded to nothing but ambient noise.

These human females sure were easy to please. Being a non-smoker with no pets that mortal eyes could see and no qualms about living in dodgy neighborhoods, I had my pick of the lot.

At some point, the screaming stopped and there was a

distant thud. Huh, I wonder what that was all—

Wow, look at this ad with the most amazing feature ever: "3 meals/day incl. I'm a culinary student and I LOVE cooking!"

My mouth watered. It would be like living in the Food Network 24/7. As a half demon, I might not *need* to eat, but I sure *liked* to. Stuffed mushrooms, seared scallops with pancetta, fluffy soufflés...

"Ahem." Someone cleared her throat from the edge of the sofa.

I jumped, sending the thick rental magazine to the floor with a *smack*.

A slender figure in a tailored, taupe business suit and genuine sea pearl necklace graced the living room with her stern feminine presence.

Crap.

It was my turn to clear my throat. A lump formed at the base of it, the blockage nonexistent just seconds ago. "Hello, Enid. I didn't hear you teleporting in."

A moment of silence.

My heart raced guiltily and I shifted my weight, feigning sudden interest in a spot on my right shoes. The image of The Machine trapped in bed, going through the routine of tears and pain without proper supervision, came to mind. Damn, talk about rotten timing. I suppose that was why they called it a *surprise* inspection. How could I not have realized I'd get into trouble the moment I stepped out of line? It'd been happening since that one time I'd tried to talk behind the teacher's back in grade two history class.

Enid was a middle-age brunette with a tightly coiled hair bun and thick-rimmed glasses. She showed off her maturity not with the tiny crow's feet around her eyes, since anyone could get them with the purchase of a bag of semi-permanent faery dust, but from the well-measured power she carried around. That kind of discipline took decades to hone, and my program mentor was a lady who meant business.

After a year of in-class lectures, students like me were eligible to join the co-op program with Enid's approval. Given the serious expression on her face right now, I needed to convince her I was responsible and reliable, which I wasn't exactly doing by being caught taking this little breather.

"Megan, in our line of work, control is an art," Enid began with quiet dignity. "Making the targets suffer just enough—"

I lifted my head. "I'm so sorry. I got a migraine and stepped out for just a mo—"

"—without scaring them to death." Enid stared at me. "Or pushing them to commit suicide."

I swallowed. "Suicide?"

Shit, what have I done? How could The Machine be dead? I left him for, like, five seconds. I'd painstakingly tested the dome-shaped barriers in the school lab. Was it my flaky magic, failing me when it most counted? Or did I overlook a procedure somewhere along the line? Didn't matter. The guy still died on my watch. Dammit.

Without another word, Enid led me into the bedroom—which was empty. She gestured towards the French doors and the balcony. "Twenty-two stories down. He landed on the concrete, poolside."

I winced. I might not have cared for the cheating bastard's lifestyle, but that didn't mean I wanted him dead. And there was his wife to think about, not to mention his newborn baby. From what I heard, it was expensive to raise kids, no matter what plane they were born into.

"You can reverse it, right?" I asked Enid urgently.

"Of course." My mentor nodded towards the window. "I've already called Reapers 'R' Us to cancel the dispatch. But you get a mark of zero in this practice session."

I wanted to kick something or cry. A mark of zero. After all the group practice sessions and hard work. I didn't realize until now that a part of me honestly thought I'd aced this with no issues. It was demoralizing to screw up in such a disastrous manner.

Alright, chin up and do some damage control. You lost the battle, but not the war. Try saying something contrite and repenting. You can't afford to fail this semester. Not if you want to move out of the dorm and get away from those dreadful girls.

"What does *he* get?" I heard myself ask. I couldn't help it. I might not want The Machine dead, but the idea of him getting off scot-free, with no memory of his punishment, didn't sit well with me, either. Maybe I just plain sucked at the whole detachment thing they valued in school.

"Something a little less...heavy." I could've sworn there was just the tiniest curve at the corners of Enid's mouth. In an instant, the facial expression made my usually austere mentor appear a decade younger.

"Like what?" Now I was intrigued.

"A period."

Vengeance Be Mine *is available at your favorite online retailers.*

Recommended reading sequence

Vengeance Be Mine (Vengeance Demons #1)

Before Vengeance (Vengeance Demons #0)

Vengeance Unclaimed (Vengeance Demons #2)

A Good Vengeance (Vengeance Demons #3)

Vengeance For Hire (Vengeance Demons #4)

Hell Hath No Vengeance (Vengeance Demons #5)

Be a Vengeful Vixen!

I'd love to have you join my Facebook reader group! Search "Vengeful Vixens Louisa Lo" on Facebook.

Sign up for my mailing list on my website for the latest news and offers!

About The Author

Louisa Lo lives in Toronto, Canada with her husband, an aristocratic cat, and more cardboard boxes than she cares to unpack. She decided to write about vigilantes, because it seems like a better life choice than trying to become one and landing herself in jail. She just has that kind of luck.

Visit Louisa's website at **www.LouisaLo.com** where you'll find her social media links.